THE UPSTANDER SUPERHEROES

Order this book online at www.trafford.com
or email orders@trafford.com

Most Trafford titles are also available at major online book retailers.

Print information available on the last page.

ISBN: 978-1-4907-6469-6 (sc)
978-1-4907-6468-9 (e)

Library of Congress Control Number: 2015914117

Trafford rev. 09/28/2015

www.trafford.com
North America & international
toll-free: 1 888 232 4444 (USA & Canada)
fax: 812 355 4082

Written by:

Elissa Ciment, M.P.H. &
Reena Rabovsky, M.S.Ed., NCSP

Illustrated by:

Rebecca Saka

For my three personal superheroes, thank you for inspiring me to write this book. I love you more than you will ever know.

—EC

I would like to dedicate the book to all the upstanders of the world, those who take action to make things right!

—RR

For my one of a kind family, thank you for everything!

—RS

Every Sunday, Charlotte and her mom went to the local supermarket to shop for groceries. Charlotte loved pushing the shopping cart and picking out brightly colored fruits and vegetables.

While shopping, Charlotte would be her mom's extra set of hands, grabbing items off the shelf, while her mom checked the items off the shopping list. They worked together as a team.

On this particular Sunday, the shopping list was extra long, and there were many items to load into the cart. As Charlotte was helping her mom push the very full and very heavy cart toward the checkout lane, she noticed her friend Olivia from school in the next aisle. Charlotte was happy to see Olivia, and she began to wave to her over the tall shopping cart.

Just as Charlotte lifted her arm to wave, something happened. She accidentally knocked over a bag of apples that was perched on top of the cart. *Uh-oh,* thought Charlotte, and she gasped as the apples went flying off the cart and down the aisles. Apples were everywhere!

Charlotte felt her cheeks getting red and her eyes welling up with tears. She turned to her mom to apologize, and just then she noticed Olivia laughing and pointing at the apples on the floor. Olivia smirked, “I can’t believe you dropped all those apples—you are such a klutz!” Charlotte’s heart sank to the floor—she felt absolutely terrible.

Suddenly, a loud whirring noise buzzed through the busy supermarket.

Everyone watched as three multicolored tornadoes of smoke came whizzing through the air, down the aisles, landing right next to Charlotte and Olivia!

Charlotte’s eyes widened as three masked superheroes appeared out of the smoke, spinning and waving their capes in the air.

“Oh my gosh!” cried Charlotte. “Who are you?”

“We are the Upstander Superheroes,” declared Superhero Sarah, who was dressed in a sparkling-blue outfit. “We are here to stand up for Charlotte!”

“We don’t just stand by when we see someone being hurt,” said Superhero Seth, who was wearing a lime green jumpsuit. “Instead, we stand up and help!”

Superhero Skylar, who was decked out in a neon-pink costume, walked over to Olivia and gently tapped her on the shoulder. “Hmm. Do you know why we are here?”

Olivia looked at the Upstander Superheros with wide eyes and shook her head back and forth. “No . . .” she said.

"It really made Charlotte feel sad and embarrassed that you laughed at her when she dropped the apples in front of everyone," said Superhero Skylar.

"But it was kind of funny," answered Olivia.

"Instead of laughing at Charlotte, what do you think you could have done?" asked Superhero Sarah.

"Well, I guess I could have comforted Charlotte or told her not to feel bad because dropping things is something that happens to everyone."

"*Yes!*" exclaimed Superhero Sarah. "Comforting is a great way to make someone feel better."

“Is there anything else you could have done?” asked Superhero Seth. Olivia looked down at the floor and thought for a moment.

“I also could have helped Charlotte pick up the apples?” suggested Olivia.

Upon hearing this, Superhero Seth waved his magic cape, and all of a sudden,

hundreds of sparkly multicolored balloons floated down from the ceiling of the supermarket.

As everyone in the supermarket became enveloped in the soft, bouncy balloons, Olivia walked over to Charlotte and gave her a hug. "I am so sorry I laughed at you—I should never have done that," said Olivia. "Especially since I drop things all the time! One time, I was helping my mom serve a bowl of grapes after dinner, and I dropped the bowl, and the grapes went flying everywhere! It took us three days to find all the grapes hiding in the kitchen corners."

Charlotte grinned. “Thank you for understanding.”

“I am so glad we are friends,” continued Charlotte. Let’s make sure never to laugh at anyone when they do something embarrassing in public.” Olivia nodded enthusiastically.

"*Yes!*" added Superhero Skylar, "And if you ever see someone act unkindly toward someone else, make sure to take action. Upstanders stand up, we do not just stand by. That is the Upstander Superhero way!"

With that, the three Upstander Superheros waved their capes, and blue, green and pink tornadoes appeared. The loud whirring noise once again buzzed through the supermarket.

“Our job here is done,” said Superhero Seth. “We are off to the next adventure.”

“Remember to always be kind to others,” added Superhero Sarah.

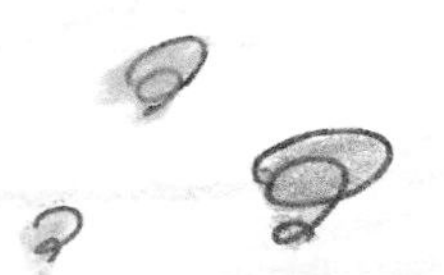

Charlotte and Olivia ran outside and watched as the Upstander Superheroes flew off into the atmosphere and kept on watching until they could not even see a speck of them in the sky. Together, the girls went back into the store and picked up the fallen apples off the floor.

When they returned to the checkout line, they saw their moms waiting for them with big smiles on their faces. “We are so glad that you learned about the importance of standing up for a friend,” said Olivia’s mom. “Now you see that being an upstander is being a hero.”

Charlotte and Olivia looked at each other and beamed.

And off they walked into the upstander fresh air.